Storie

C000059106

The Dream

Siân Lewis

Illustrated by James Field

The Dream

That day, even though I am Welsh, I wanted to be a soldier of the King of England.

I was ten.

And I was hurt.

I had gashed my left elbow, when I was helping my father and brothers in the fields. Even after my sister had bound it with a rag, it was still painful.

With the rag on my arm I pretended I was a soldier who had been wounded in battle. I had fought so well that King Henry had said, 'Here you are, Sir Rhys. For being so brave, I am making you the new constable of Harlech castle.'

My father had given me a day off, so I marched up into the hills and set up a sentry post on a small ledge beneath an overhanging bush. The rocks were my castle walls and I guarded them with my wooden sword.

From my hiding place I could see the tiny figures of my father and brothers toiling in the fields below. I pointed my sword at them. 'Get back to your hovels, you filthy dogs!' I growled in the voice of the constable of Harlech.

The constable had shouted those very words at my father and my brother Hywel, when they went to sell apples and eggs at the castle gate. Though my father and brother couldn't speak the constable's language, they understood his meaning well enough by the tone of his voice. I didn't know what those words meant either, till Lame Gruffudd told me.

Lame Gruffudd had once fought for the King of England and was always bragging about the good money and the good food.

I hadn't brought any food with me that day. That was stupid. You should always have a store of food in a castle. By midday I was starving. I was so hungry I had decided to go down the hill to look for ground nuts, when I saw four soldiers come galloping from the direction of Harlech. On my ledge I gripped both ends of the sword and pretended I was galloping too. It was better than being a sentry. I was riding like the wind without moving an inch, when I realised the soldiers were heading straight for me.

'Halt! Halt!' they shouted.

Halt? What had I done wrong? I tried to remember all those things that Welshmen were forbidden to do. I hadn't entered the garrison town of Harlech except on market day. I hadn't tried to buy land or property in the town. I hadn't carried arms, unless they counted my wooden sword. I dropped the sword as if it were on fire and began to crawl from under the bush. But as soon as I poked my nose out, I saw that I was not alone on the hillside. Making his way along the track below me, almost invisible against the rocks, was a monk in a grey cloak. I could see his white face. I saw too the sack that slid from his hand and fell among the stones.

I ducked back. I was safe after all. The soldiers were chasing the monk, not me.

'Halt, you holy fool!' they shouted.

Despite the noise, the monk walked calmly, quietly, on

5

his way. Even when the riders caught up with him he did not make a sound. The first soldier reached down and knocked him to the ground. The others leapt from their saddles, shouted at the monk and hit him. Then they picked him up, threw him over a horse and galloped back towards Harlech.

When they had gone and the dust had settled, I slid down the slope to look for the monk's sack. I found it easily. Inside was a loaf of bread and dried salt fish. I took the sack back up to my hiding place and ate the fish. I ate and ate till my stomach was full; then to my shame I fell asleep at my post.

I was woken by deep voices and the clanking of spurs and swords. Six more soldiers had dismounted below me and were searching among the rocks where the sack had fallen. Now I was twice as scared as I had been before. My breath was stinking of fish. If that fish belonged to the King of England, the soldiers would surely whip me half to death for eating it. I put a stone in my mouth and sucked hard to get rid of the smell.

Below me the noise stopped. Through the branches of the bush I saw the soldiers shade their eyes and gaze all around them at the bare hilltops. They were looking for someone. I hoped it wasn't me. I hoped it was an enemy of the King of England.

After many minutes the leader of the soldiers turned to the others and shrugged, as if to say, 'There's nowhere for a man to hide up there.'

He was wrong. Up above me, behind an outcrop of rock, was a cave that Gethin the poacher used when the constable's men were after him. It was invisible from below and could only be reached along a narrow ledge.

Beneath me I could feel the round shape of the loaf, which was all that remained of the food in the monk's sack. The monks have always despised King Henry and will do all they can to oppose him. That monk had been bringing food for an enemy of the King, I was sure of it. And I was sure I knew where that enemy was hiding too. The King's men would never find him unless I showed them the way. If I did, they would have to reward me.

In my hurry to claim my reward, I forgot my wounded arm. As I pushed myself up, the pain tore through my body and made me fall in a faint. By the time I came to my senses the soldiers had returned to their horses. 'Rise up, Sir Rhys,' I urged myself.

So I rose. I dragged myself out from under the bush, but the soldiers were already riding away. I was alone.

Down below, the tiny figures of my father and brothers were still bent-backed and cutting the reeds. I didn't want to scratch and slave. I wanted to make my fortune. That was my dream. If I found the King's enemy and handed him over to the soldiers, then maybe I too could be a soldier and make that dream come true. I picked up the sack and my sword, tucked both into my belt and began to crawl up the slope like a dog with a broken leg.

Soon I was panting noisily like a dog too. That's why I didn't hear the enemy.

When I reached the outcrop of rock, a man reared up, a giant of a man with blazing eyes. He put one hand around my neck and a hand across my panting mouth. I bit him hard, as hard as I could, till he let me go.

'You young wolf!' he growled.

'You were hurting me,' I said, dodging his outstretched arm. 'It's not fair to hurt me, when I've come with food for you.'

The enemy was older than my father. Though his clothes had once been fine, they were stained and torn. He watched me take the sack from my belt.

'A monk left this for you,' I said.

'Who was he?'

'I don't know. He was captured by soldiers and taken to Harlech.'

'To Harlech?' The tall man looked over my shoulder. I turned. In the distance, below us, was Harlech castle. It shone like the sun itself on its pinnacle of rock. At its base frothed the sea. 'One day I shall be in Harlech castle,' the man said.

I said nothing. I was wary. I thought the tall man could read my thoughts and knew that he'd end up as a prisoner because of me. He had the look of a prophet or poet. The King of England hates prophets and poets. He says they go around filling people's heads with ideas they have no right to hold.

'I shall be Lord of Harlech,' said the tall man.

So he hadn't read my mind at all. I laughed. How could an enemy of the King of England be Lord of Harlech castle?

His eyes burned as though he had a fever. 'I shall lead a Welsh army that will capture Harlech and all other castles in Wales,' he said. 'This whole land will be yours and mine. We Welsh shall govern our land according to our own laws in our own language. We shall have a church that our poor friends the monks can call their own and a college where you shall study to be a wise man. What do you say to that, young fish-breath?'

I said nothing. He was hungry and he was opening the sack. It didn't take much of a prophet to know that there was no fish inside. It didn't matter. In the ground beneath my feet I could feel the tremble of horses' hoofs. More soldiers were coming. If the tall man got angry, all I had to do was slide down the slope and shout to them. He would never escape. He had nowhere to go. His fate was in my hands. I ruled him.

But the tall man did not get angry. He took out the loaf from the sack, peeped inside, sniffed and laughed. Then he broke a piece of the loaf and gave it to me. 'Never let it be said that I turned you away hungry from my door,' he said.

I couldn't say a word. He had stuffed a chunk of bread into my mouth! He was holding my good arm. The horsemen rode by.

When they had gone, he let go of me. 'Off you go, young soldier,' he said.

I went, but I forgot my sword. As I was sliding down the slope, I heard a clatter behind me and there was my sword swooping over the rocks. I stuck it in my belt and saw the tall man raise his hand. I did not wave back.

In the distance I could see another crowd of horsemen leaving Harlech castle.

I would meet them on my way home.

I told no one the story of that day. How could I? My brothers would have been angry with me. I can hardly believe myself that I was such a fool. Did I really want to be a soldier of the King of England? So much has happened since that day. Owain Glyndŵr is the man to fight for now. Owain Glyndŵr, Prince of Wales.

The first time I heard his name was one misty spring morning. We were all woken by a low roar, as if the earth itself was on fire. We ran outside and saw a crowd of Welshmen settle around Harlech castle. They stayed there long enough to scare the constable and then like the mist they were gone.

My father was overjoyed.

'It's a sign of what's to come,' he said. 'Those Welshmen are led by a man called Owain Glyndŵr. Remember his name, Rhys. It's a name that already strikes fear into the heart of the King of England.'

'Why?' I asked, because I could not imagine the King being afraid.

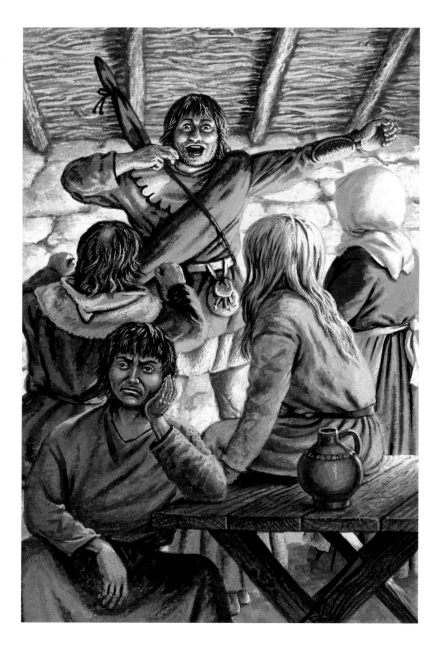

'King Henry has taken our land,' my father said. 'He has passed laws which make us foreigners in our own country. We cannot sell our goods in the towns. Owain Glyndŵr will change all that. He will make us proud again and Wales will take its place among the free nations of the world.'

That night, when I was asleep, my brother Hywel left home. He went to join the army of Owain Glyndŵr.

I was furious.

'Why didn't he tell me?' I said. 'I could have gone too. I'm the one who wants to be a soldier, not him.'

My sister Gwenllian laughed. 'You and your wooden sword,' she said.

My wooden sword was just a toy. I hadn't played with it for a year or more. Instead I had made myself a longbow from a yew branch. With my bow I sent twigs arcing through the air like the comet that blazed through the sky that spring.

'The comet will bring luck to Owain Glyndŵr, you mark my words,' my father said.

He was right. After many months my brother returned, proud and boastful.

'I have fought a battle at Bryn Glas on the English border,' he said. 'We were only a small band, but we drove back the army of the English King. You should have seen our arrows winging through the air.'

'I can shoot arrows,' I said.

No one listened. They only had ears for Hywel.

'I was the one who wanted to be soldier,' I said.

'So you shall,' replied my mother. 'But not yet. You will have to wait.'

'How long?' I said. 'Owain Glyndŵr is sweeping through Wales from north to south. All the castles are crumbling before him. Soon there will be nothing left to fight for.'

'There is still Harlech,' said my father.

As he spoke he looked up at the strong fortress on the cliff top. On its tower stood the standard of the English King, trembling as if it really were afraid.

At long last the night came when our sleep was disturbed by rustlings, the clinking of swords, the soft snuffle of horses, the pawing of hoofs. The noise welled up around us. It grew as loud as the roar of a stormy sea. Owain Glyndŵr had returned.

By morning Harlech castle was under siege. Owain Glyndŵr and his men had camped around it. Hywel was one of them. For weeks they stayed there. No food was allowed in. Slowly the constable and his men began to starve. I thought of that constable driving my father and brothers away and thought how pleased he'd be to buy their eggs and apples now.

One warm evening, long after the siege had begun, I was going back to the house from the fields when Gethin the poacher came by with a sack on his back.

'Hey, Rhys,' he said to me. 'Come up the hill with me.'

'Why?' I said. 'You don't have to hide any more. The

constable of Harlech can't do anything to you, can he?'

'No.' Gethin laughed. 'The constable of Harlech is the one who's hiding now. Maybe tonight we'll see him flushed from his hole.'

I went with him that evening. We sat on the slope near where the tall man had hidden. The sun was a great burning ball sinking into the sea. Its beams flickered along the walls of Harlech castle.

Through those flames we saw a strange and wonderful sight. We saw the great door of the castle open. We saw the drawbridge lowered. Into the castle rushed a joyful crowd of those people who for so long had been kept out. They swarmed along the battlements, their shouts echoing from hill to hill.

Then Gethin the poacher threw back his head and roared with delight. He crushed me in his arms. He danced around with fire in his eyes.

'We have taken Harlech castle!' Gethin cried. He punched me on the shoulder. 'We are lords of Harlech. Don't you understand?'

'Yes,' I replied.

'Then look happy, man. What's the matter with you? Hey, you're jealous of your brother Hywel, aren't you, because he's there in the thick of it helping Owain Glyndŵr?'

I smiled for Gethin's sake. I couldn't tell him that I had once met another fiery-eyed man in that very place. I was only ten then, a boy with a wooden sword. I couldn't tell him about the choice I had made that day, because he wouldn't

have understood why I had to make a choice at all.

My brother Hywel was made stable hand to Owain Glyndŵr in his castle at Harlech. None of us had yet set eyes on the Prince, except from a distance, so Hywel liked to show off how much he knew. He would point up at the castle and say, 'That is the tower where Prince Owain and his wife Marged live. In the hall there's a great throne on which the prince sits when he talks to important people from Wales and Ireland, Scotland and France. Soon he will call a parliament of the people of Wales in that very place.'

I was tired of Hywel's bragging and of his teasing too.

'The Prince is going to hold a tournament,' my brother said. 'You can all come and see it.' He slapped me on the back. 'You'll like that, Rhys, though it's not proper fighting, of course.'

'Huh!' I replied.

Anyone would think that Hywel had single-handedly driven the King's men away from Harlech castle. I wanted to pretend I wasn't interested in the tournament, but that was impossible. There was so much excitement in the air. Brightly coloured tents were set up on the green and the knights began to arrive in town in their plumes and fine armour. To show their bravery some of the knights had lions on their shields, but none had as many as Owain Glyndŵr.

'Owain Glyndŵr has four lions on his shield,' said Hywel.

I knew that. Gethin had told me. They were four fierce

lions rampant, each one standing up on a hind leg and pawing the air.

On the day of the tournament I hurried to the green and looked all around me for Owain Glyndŵr. My father pointed out Marged, Princess of Wales, in the royal tent. Beside her was an empty throne. My head was turning this way and that, when a great roar ran through the crowd. A black knight had ridden into the jousting ring and who should be facing him but a shining figure, his face hidden by a helmet. On the man's arm was a shield with four lions rampant.

'It's Owain Glyndŵr!' breathed the crowd. 'The Prince himself is going to take part in the tournament.'

With a blaring of trumpets the Black Knight and the Prince took up their positions.

'Owain! Owain! Owain!' we all chanted till our voices were drowned by the thunder of hoofs, the clang of metal. We gasped, we shouted, we sighed as their lances were splintered. Both men were unseated and fought each other on foot with clashing swords. My father and I shrank back as the fight came towards us and sparks flew all around.

Right there at our feet, with one last clang, the Black Knight fell. Owain stood over him with his sword pointing at his throat.

The crowd was hushed and I was catching my breath, when I heard Owain's voice.

'So, young fish-breath,' it said. 'We meet again.'

I looked up with a start.

The Prince had removed his helmet and there, gazing

at me, were the sharp eyes of the tall man of the hills.

'Tell me,' he said. 'What shall I do with this beaten knight? Shall I throw him to his enemies or let him go?'

I said nothing. My mouth was dry.

'Come on,' said Owain. 'The decision is yours.'

'Then let him go,' I said.

Let him go. That was my decision that day. It had also been my decision long ago when I was ten years old. I had never betrayed the tall man of the hills. On my way home I had passed the King's soldiers without a word. Why? Because I knew even then that his dream was so much greater and more glorious than mine.

Owain Glyndŵr, great Prince of Wales, smiled at me.

'Well done,' he said and he touched my shoulder with the flat blade of his sword.